Kirk Parrish (illustrator) grew up on a little island just off the coast of Seattle, Washington. As a youngster, he developed a fondness for scribbling caped superheroes and yearned to one day become a grand-master ninja. Today, Parrish has (mostly) put down his ninja aspirations and is an illustrator and designer, currently based in Seattle. Over the last decade, his artwork has appeared in video games, animation, publishing, and advertising.

"Move the Crowd"
Written by Eric Barrier and William Griffin
Courtesy of Universal Songs of PolyGram International, Inc., on behalf of itself, and Robert Hill Music
Used by Permission. All Rights Reserved.

LyricPop is a children's picture book collection by LyricVerse and Akashic Books.

Published by Akashic Books
Song lyrics ©1987 Written by Eric Barrier and William Griffin
Illustrations ©2020 Kirk Parrish

ISBN: 978-1-61775-849-2
Library of Congress Control Number: 2020935822
First printing

Printed in China

Akashic Books
Brooklyn, New York
Twitter: @AkashicBooks
Facebook: AkashicBooks
E-mail: info@akashicbooks.com
Website: www.akashicbooks.com

song lyrics by **ERIC BARRIER** and **WILLIAM GRIFFIN**
illustrations by **KIRK PARRISH**

 AKASHIC BOOKS LYRICPOP

Standing by the speaker,

suddenly I had this

FEVER,
was it me
or either
summer madness

So I get closer

and the closer I get,

the

BETTER

it

sound

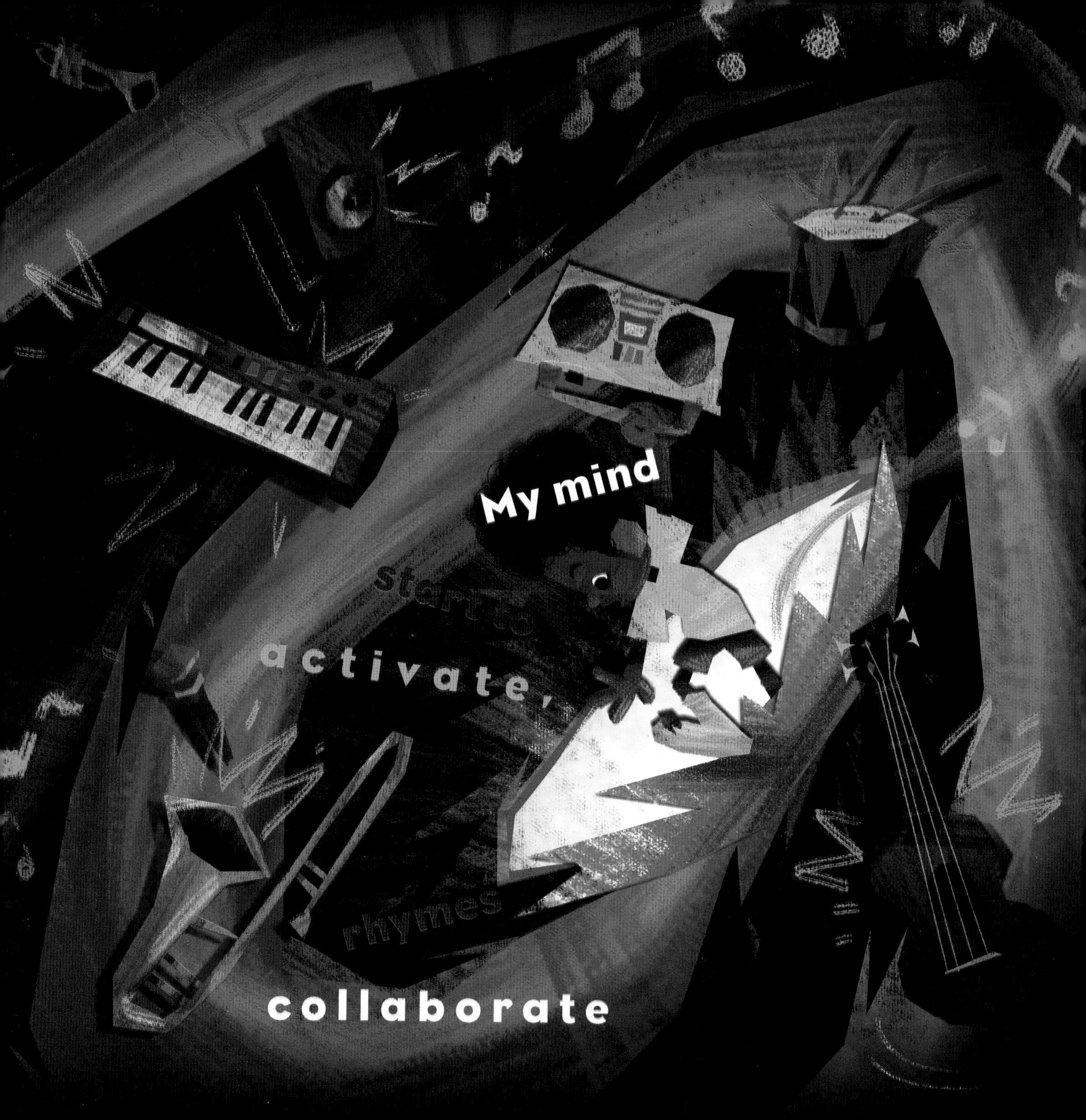

My mind

start to

activate,

rhymes

collaborate

'Cause when I heard the beat
I just HAD to make
Something from the top of my head

**So I fell into the groove
of the wax and I said**

How could I MOVE THE CROWD?

First of all, ain't no mistakes allowed

Here's the instruction, **put it together**

It's simple ain't it, but quite clever

Is this the BEST that you can make?
'Cause if not and you got more, I'll wait
But don't make me wait too long
'cause I'ma move on

The dance floor when they put somethin' smooth on
So turn up the bass, it's better when it's LOUD
'Cause I like to move the crowd

Imagine me with the heat
that's made by solar
It gets stronger every time I hold a

Microphone, check the tone to get started

The line for the microphone is departed

Your hands in the air, your mouth is shut
'Cause I'm on the mic
and Eric B. is on the cut

For those
that know me,
indeed I like
to flow
Especially when
the music's going
slow

It gives me a chance to let everybody know It's time to bust out the Rakim show

I'm the intelligent
wise on the mic I will rise
Right in front of your eyes
'cause I am a surprise
So I'ma let my knowledge
be born to a perfection
All praises due to Allah
and that's a blessing

With knowledge of self,
there's nothing I can't solve
At three hundred and sixty
degrees I revolve

This is actual fact, it's not an act, it's been proven

Indeed and I proceed to make the crowd

KEEP MOVING

LOOK OUT FOR THESE LyricPop TITLES

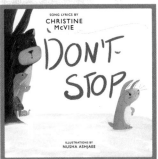

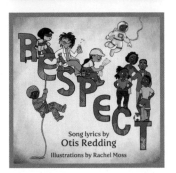

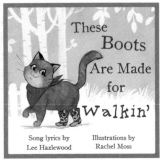

African SONG LYRICS BY PETER TOSH
ILLUSTRATIONS BY RACHEL MOSS

(Sittin' on) The Dock of the Bay
SONG LYRICS BY OTIS REDDING AND STEVE CROPPER
ILLUSTRATIONS BY KAITLYN SHEA O'CONNOR

Don't Stop SONG LYRICS BY CHRISTINE McVIE
ILLUSTRATIONS BY NUSHA ASHJAEE

Good Vibrations
SONG LYRICS BY MIKE LOVE AND BRIAN WILSON
ILLUSTRATIONS BY PAUL HOPPE

Humble and Kind SONG LYRICS BY LORI McKENNA
ILLUSTRATIONS BY KATHERINE BLACKMORE

Respect SONG LYRICS BY OTIS REDDING
ILLUSTRATIONS BY RACHEL MOSS

These Boots Are Made for Walkin'
SONG LYRICS BY LEE HAZLEWOOD
ILLUSTRATIONS BY RACHEL MOSS

We Got the Beat SONG LYRICS BY CHARLOTTE CAFFEY
ILLUSTRATIONS BY KAITLYN SHEA O'CONNOR

We're Not Gonna Take It SONG LYRICS BY DEE SNIDER
ILLUSTRATIONS BY MARGARET McCARTNEY